To my father Ken—
thank you for my love
of languages and thirst
for knowledge.
K.W.-M.

Consultants: Paulette Nhlapo
Said el-Gheithy
Centre for African Language Learning.
Mavuso Tshabalala

For information address
Hyperion Books for Children,
114 Fifth Avenue,
New York, 10011-5690.

First Edition
1 3 5 7 9 10 8 6 4 2

ISBN 0-7868-0414-9

Production by Imago.

Printed in Singapore

Library of Congress Catalog No: 98-11003

Full Library of Congress
Cataloging-in-Publication Data on file.

Halala Means Welcome!
A Book of Zulu Words

Written and illustrated by
Ken Wilson-Max

Hyperion Books for Children
New York

Africa

South Africa

Welcome to South Africa.

Africa is a large continent where many people live. South Africa is one of its 52 countries.

Chidi and Michael are friends. They live in South Africa. They speak Zulu (Zoo-loo), a musical language that is fun to learn.

When Chidi and Michael greet each other, they say *halala* (ha-la-la), which means welcome in Zulu. Now, they welcome you to their world by introducing their Zulu language. Check the word listing in the back of the book to see how to say the words correctly.

Welcome to South Africa. Halala!

Chidi  Michael

Hello! My name is Chidi. My friend Michael came to my house today. I waited for him near the flowers by the door.

I said "Halala!" which means welcome.

"Hello!" he said. I've brought some toys in my bag for us to play with."

Door **Umnyango**

House **Indlu**

Toy car **Umgqukumbane**

Flowers **Izimbali**

When we went to my room, I showed Michael my map and my shelf full of books. Michael opened his bag and took out the toy car he'd brought to show me. We had fun driving cars off the edge of my desk. Then I showed him the ball from under my bed.

Ball **Ibhola**

Bag **Umgodla**

Desk **Idesiki**

Bed **Umbhede**

Books **Amabhuku**

Map **Imephu**

Africa

We went into the kitchen for a snack. My mother put two plates, silverware, and a jug of milk out on the table. I wanted to drink milk out of my favorite red mug. I showed Michael some colorful bottles that I had decorated with beads.

Mother Umama

Mug Inkomishi

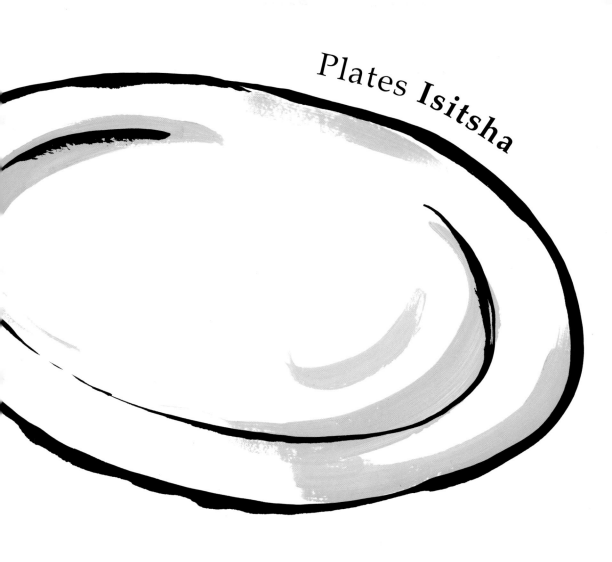

Plates Isitsha

Milk Ubisi

I took Michael outside to our vegetable garden where I watered the tomato plants. We even milked the goat and fed the hens. One of the hens had laid an egg!

Hen Isikhukhukazi

Egg Iqanda

Goat Imbuzi

Tomato Utamatisi

Water Amanzi

Michael and I had so much fun that I didn't want my friend to leave. But soon he had to catch the bus home.

"I hope you can come to my house next weekend, Chidi," Michael said as he got on the bus.

"I can't wait," I said. "Goodbye!"

The big wheels started turning and the noisy bus pulled away.

Bus **Ibhasi**

Wheel **Isondo**

Friends **Abangane**

Goodbye! **Hamba kahle!**

How to Say the words

All the words in this book are easy to say if you split the words into single parts. These parts are called **syllables**. Each syllable has its own sound. Some syllables are called stressed syllables. These are the syllables shown in italics in the word list opposite. They are louder and longer than normal syllables.

Vowels are important in most languages and appear in most words. The vowels are **a**, **e**, **i**, **o**, and **u**. They sound like this:
a as in b**a**rk, **e** as in r**ei**gn, **i** as in p**ie**ce, **o** as in b**o**rn, and **u** as in r**u**le.

The letter **q**, as in **iqanda** (egg), is said by putting your tongue on the roof of your mouth and clicking it, just like making a tutting sound.

The letters **bh** together sound like a **b**.

Learning new words in any language takes time and practice. Ask an adult to help you, and have fun!

Bag .... **Um-*god*-la**

Ball .... **I-*bho*-la**

Bed .... **Um-*bhe*-de**

Books .... **A-ma-*bhu*-ku**

Bus .... **I-*bha*-si**

Desk .... **I-de-*si*-ki**

Door .... **Um-*nyan*-go**

Egg .... **I-*qan*-da**

Flowers .... **I-zim-*ba*-li**

Friends .... **A-bang-*a*-ne**

Goat .... **Im-*bu*-zi**

Goodbye .... *Ham*-ba *ka*-hle

Hello .... *Saw*-ubona

Hen .... **I-si-khu-khu-*ka*-zi**

House .... *Ind*-lu

Map .... **I-*mep*-hu**

Milk .... **U-*bi*-si**

Mother .... **U-*ma*-ma**

Mug .... **In-ko-*mi*-shi**

Plates .... **I-*sit*-sha**

Tomato .... **U-ta-ma-*ti*-si**

Toy car .... **Um-g-qu-k-um-*ba*-ne**

Water .... **A-*man*-zi**

Welcome .... **Ha-la-la**

Wheels .... **I-*son*-do**